SPORTS GREAT
JIM
KELLY

—Sports Great Books—

Sports Great Jim Abbott
(ISBN 0-89490-395-0)

Sports Great Troy Aikman
(ISBN 0-89490-593-7)

Sports Great Charles Barkley
(ISBN 0-89490-386-1)

Sports Great Larry Bird
(ISBN 0-89490-368-3)

Sports Great Barry Bonds
(ISBN 0-89490-595-3)

Sports Great Bobby Bonilla
(ISBN 0-89490-417-5)

Sports Great Roger Clemens
(ISBN 0-89490-284-9)

Sports Great John Elway
(ISBN 0-89490-282-2)

Sports Great Patrick Ewing
(ISBN 0-89490-369-1)

Sports Great Steffi Graf
(ISBN 0-89490-597-X)

Sports Great Orel Hershiser
(ISBN 0-89490-389-6)

Sports Great Bo Jackson
(ISBN 0-89490-281-4)

**Sports Great Magic Johnson
(Revised and Expanded)**
(ISBN 0-89490-348-9)

Sports Great Michael Jordan
(ISBN 0-89490-370-5)

Sports Great Jim Kelly
(ISBN 0-89490-670-4)

Sports Great Mario Lemieux
(ISBN 0-89490-596-1)

Sports Great Karl Malone
(ISBN 0-89490-599-6)

Sports Great Joe Montana
(ISBN 0-89490-371-3)

Sports Great Hakeem Olajuwon
(ISBN 0-89490-372-1)

Sports Great Shaquille O'Neal
(ISBN 0-89490-594-5)

Sports Great Kirby Puckett
(ISBN 0-89490-392-6)

Sports Great Jerry Rice
(ISBN 0-89490-419-1)

Sports Great Cal Ripken, Jr.
(ISBN 0-89490-387-X)

Sports Great David Robinson
(ISBN 0-89490-373-X)

Sports Great Nolan Ryan
(ISBN 0-89490-394-2)

Sports Great Barry Sanders
(ISBN 0-89490-418-3)

Sports Great John Stockton
(ISBN 0-89490-598-8)

Sports Great Darryl Strawberry
(ISBN 0-89490-291-1)

Sports Great Isiah Thomas
(ISBN 0-89490-374-8)

Sports Great Herschel Walker
(ISBN 0-89490-207-5)

SPORTS GREAT
JIM
KELLY

Denis J. Harrington

—Sports Great Books—

ENSLOW PUBLISHERS, INC.

44 Fadem Road	P.O. Box 38
Box 699	Aldershot
Springfield, N.J. 07081	Hants GU12 6 BP
U.S.A.	U.K.

Library of Congress Cataloging-in-Publication Data

Harrington, Denis J., 1932-
    Sports great Jim Kelly / Denis J. Harrington.
       p. cm. — (Sports great books)
    Includes index.
    Summary: Examines the life and football career of the
    quarterback for the Buffalo Bills, Jim Kelly.
    ISBN 0-89490-670-4
    1. Kelly, Jim, 1960– —Juvenile literature. 2. Football players—United
States—Biography—Juvenile literature. 3. Buffalo Bills (Football team)—Juvenile literature.
[1. Kelly, Jim, 1960– . 2. Football players.] I. Title. II. Series.
GV939.K87H37 1995
796.332'092 B—dc20

                            95-14144
                               CIP
                               AC

Photo Credits: © Copyright 1994 Jim Bush, pp. 6, 11, 16, 18, 32, 35, 39, 42, 45,
47, 51, 53, 55, 57, 60; University of Miami Sports Information Office, pp. 21, 25,
26, 29.

Cover Photo: © Copyright 1994 Jim Bush

Contents

Chapter 1 7

Chapter 2 13

Chapter 3 20

Chapter 4 31

Chapter 5 41

Chapter 6 49

Career Statistics 62

Where to Write 62

Index 63

Kelly decided to try a no-huddle offense during the entire game against the Eagles. Even though his coaches doubted him, the Bills won the game with this strategy.

Chapter 1

On December 2, 1990, more than seventy-nine thousand fans filled Rich Stadium in New York. They roared their greeting as the Buffalo Bills trotted onto the field. The welcome was heartfelt because, going into game twelve of the regular season, the Bills boasted a 9–2 record. In fact, the team was already looking forward to the playoffs. So the cheering came easy. But no one could have guessed just how easy the win would be that day.

As the Bills crossed the artificial turf, quarterback Jim Kelly studied the Philadelphia Eagles along the opposite sideline. His eyes went right to big defensive ends Reggie White and Clyde Simmons, huge defensive tackle Jerome Brown, and linebacker Seth Joyner. These players formed the best pass-rushing combination in the National Football League (NFL). Kelly knew that they would be in his face all afternoon. But he also knew something that they didn't know.

The Eagles kicked off, and the Bills' runner returned the ball to the team's thirty-four-yard line. On the first play from scrimmage, Kelly handed off to ace running mate Thurman

Thomas. Thomas carried the ball for three yards to the thirty-seven-yard line. Then, instead of going to a huddle, the Bills went right to the next play.

Before the Philadelphia players could get set, Kelly took the snap from center and dropped back to pass. With his blockers holding firm, he looked for an open receiver downfield. In a matter of moments he saw wideout James Lofton break free. So he threw deep to his teammate. Lofton caught the ball without breaking stride and easily outran the Eagles' secondary. Touchdown, Buffalo! While using only 45 seconds of playing time, the Bills had moved 66 yards and scored to go ahead, 7–0. Unfortunately for the Eagles, this was just the beginning.

As the Buffalo defensive unit took over, Kelly settled down on the bench. He caught the eye of defensive coordinator Ted Marchibroda. They exchanged knowing glances. For some time Kelly had thought that the no-huddle offense would work for an entire game. Marchibroda was not quite as certain—Kelly had to convince him. Head coach Marv Levy didn't like the idea all that much either.

In the Bills' playbook the no-huddle offense was code-named "K-Gun." Basically, it was designed as a two-minute drill, the objective being to get the ball into scoring position as quickly as possible. Under this system Kelly called his own plays, running one right after the other. The offense worked very well when Buffalo was behind with the game clock ticking down.

Kelly felt sure that the K-Gun series would be just as effective if used regularly. At every opportunity he made this argument to Marchibroda. But the response was always, "I don't know about that, Jim." Still, Kelly kept at it. Gradually the no-huddle offense became a bigger part of the Bills' weekly game plan. It never failed to put points on the scoreboard in a hurry.

Marchibroda finally agreed to run the K-Gun full-time against Philadelphia. He felt it might work well against the Eagles, because this team liked to blitz a lot. With no time between plays the Eagles' linebackers would be hard-pressed to keep pace with the fast-moving Bills. Right now the offense was working just as Kelly had thought.

When Buffalo got the ball again, Kelly kept up the pressure. He mixed short passes with Thurman Thomas's running to move his team into Philadelphia territory once more. A few plays later, placekicker Scott Norwood booted a 43-yard field goal. The Bills now led, 10–0, with the first quarter not yet half over!

Back on the bench, Kelly stared at the Eagles across the field. Some members of the defense sat with their heads down. He knew that they were not only discouraged, but tired. Tired from chasing him and trying to keep up with Buffalo's nonstop attack. The K-Gun had already proven itself.

The next time the Bills got their hands on the ball, they offered more of the same. Kelly took the snap at the Buffalo thirty-five and handed off to Thomas. Behind good blocking, Thomas banged his way to the forty-four, for a gain of nine yards. Now only one yard was needed for a first down. Quickly the Philadelphia defenders bunched themselves to stop another thrust into the line. They couldn't have been more wrong.

Kelly retreated from the snap and faked a handoff to Thomas. He then directed his gaze downfield. Wide receiver Andre Reed was in a foot race with the man covering him. Kelly knew Reed would win the contest. He put the ball up high and deep. Reed stretched to his full height and gathered in the pass. The two connected for a 56-yard touchdown play. Now the Bills were ahead, 17–0.

After just twenty-seven seconds of work, Kelly turned toward the Buffalo sideline once again. Suddenly he heard a deep voice in his ear. It was the Eagles' Jerome Brown. "Come on, slow it down, man," he huffed and puffed. "What are you trying to do, kill us?"

Kelly merely grinned and kept walking. Inside he thought, "This is fun. What a great feeling."

Less than three minutes remained in the quarter when Buffalo began its fourth drive of the game. On third down at his own twenty-five, Kelly dropped back, looking for a receiver going deep. He saw Lofton running a curling post route and led him with the ball. The sure-handed wideout made the catch before being brought down at the Philadelphia four-yard line. With this 71-yard reception, the Bills were in position for yet another score.

When Kelly took the next snap he simply stood tall and pitched a perfect strike to Thomas in the Eagles' end zone. The Bills went up, 24–0, with a minute still left in the first period. At that point Kelly had connected with all 8 of his passes for 229 yards and 3 TDs.

Philadelphia mounted a strong comeback in the second quarter, cutting Buffalo's lead to 24–16 at halftime. But Kelly and his teammates felt confident that they could hang on for the win. "We weren't making any mistakes," he said, looking back at the first 30 minutes of the game. "We were just on a huge roll. And the feeling was we could keep it going in the last half."

The Eagles took the opening kickoff of the third quarter and drove for another touchdown. Now the Bills led by just the narrowest of margins, 24–23. But they didn't panic. Kelly stayed with the no-huddle offense and kept making the big plays when needed. His 35-yard completion to Thomas put

Norwood in position to kick a 21-yard field goal. Buffalo inched ahead, 27–23.

When Philadelphia threatened to score again, the Bills' defense came to the rescue with a pass interception. Once more Kelly relied upon the K-Gun to move his team into enemy territory. The result was a 45-yard field goal. Now Buffalo had more breathing room, 30–23.

Late in the fourth period Kelly showed why he is known as "Mr. Clutch" among NFL quarterbacks. When the Bills took possession of the ball at the Philadelphia forty-nine-yard line, he set about using up the clock. He mixed runs with passes to keep the Eagles' defense off balance. When a first down was needed, he threaded an 8-yard completion to Lofton at the thirty-eight-yard line. Minutes later Kelly kept the drive alive with a 7-yard pitch to Reed. And so the game went until only 13 seconds were left. This was not enough time for the Eagles to muster a rally. The 30–23 victory moved Buffalo a step closer to the Super Bowl.

Kelly is free and clear to pass. The Eagles' defensive team could not touch him during this game!

Overall, Kelly connected on 19 of 32 passes for 334 yards—his best performance of the season. Much of the credit for this fine showing had to do with his not being sacked.

"Whenever Philadelphia blitzed I would get free and hit the open receiver," he said. "If someone had told me beforehand that I wasn't going to be under a pile of Eagles at least three or four times during the game I'd have thought they were goofy."

The no-huddle offense was a success. It had kept the likes of White, Simmons, Brown, and Joyner scrambling to adjust all afternoon. They simply weren't allowed to get an organized pass rush going with any degree of consistency. "Averaging 18 to 20 seconds between snaps really agreed with me," Kelly said. "I'm the kind of person who's constantly doing something. From the time I wake up in the morning, I'm on fast forward. That's just my way."

He also liked calling his own plays. Making decisions was something that had come naturally to him from his earliest days in football.

"Even when playing in the midget leagues as a kid," he said, "I didn't mind having full responsibility for the offense. The buck should stop at the quarterback. And that's how I want it."

Pro football has experienced a lot of change in its seventy-five-year history. But playing an entire game without huddling between downs had been thought to be unworkable. That was before Sunday, December 2, 1990, when Kelly and the Buffalo Bills made believers out of everybody.

Chapter 2

Jim Kelly was born on February 14, 1960, at St. Francis Hospital in Pittsburgh, Pennsylvania. Alice and Joe Kelly considered him to be the best Valentine's Day present that they ever received. Later his mother would say, "Not even Hallmark™ has one as good."

Alice and Joe had six sons, with Jim being the fourth oldest. Because of the boys, the family home in East Brady—a small working-class town some sixty-five miles northeast of Pittsburgh—was always active. The boys got involved with sports as soon as they were old enough. During bad weather the living room served as an indoor stadium.

Cutoff plastic containers stapled to the walls and a pair of rolled-up socks enabled them to play basketball. At other times they put on football helmets. The three older brothers—Pat, Ed, and Ray—lined up against the three younger ones—Jim, Danny, and Kevin. With the couch serving as the end zone, they took turns trying to score a touchdown. Such games took a heavy toll on the furniture and on Alice Kelly's nerves. "I always said I wouldn't trade my boys for anything," she once recalled, "but there were days I would have gladly given them away."

During these rough-and-tumble contests tempers would sometimes flare and punches would fly. On such occasions Joe Kelly took the boys out to the garage. There he had them put on football helmets and boxing gloves to settle their differences. When they were tired of swinging he made them shake hands, finishing as friends.

Joe Kelly was employed as a machinist in a local plant. To help make ends meet, he did carpentry work after-hours and on weekends.

But Joe Kelly still found time to coach his sons. His knowledge of the various sports came from studying library books. He also took the boys to East Brady High School at every opportunity. There they could see how the games were played firsthand.

Each son started organized football with the North Butler County Midget Football League. Jim's turn came when he was eight years old. Because of his large size, he became a tight end. At this position, he didn't get much chance to handle the ball. The next year the coaches moved him to quarterback. He quickly fell in love with this new position and began to dream of a future in football.

At age ten, he reached the semifinals of the national Punt, Pass, and Kick competition. The following year he repeated as the Pittsburgh regional champion. Before the ceremonies began at Three Rivers Stadium, he got to meet Steelers' quarterback Terry Bradshaw—his boyhood hero. They shook hands, and Jim said, "I'm going to take your job away, Mr. Bradshaw." Even then, Jim wanted to play pro football.

During junior high school Jim Kelly practiced passing and kicking almost every day under the watchful eye of his father. He also worked on such quarterbacking techniques as taking snaps, pivoting, and sprinting out of the pocket. As his arm became stronger he was able to throw longer and with more force. Soon the ball was stinging the hands of his receivers.

When not practicing on his own, Jim played pickup basketball and backyard whiffleball with his brothers and friends. In the winter months they added ice hockey to their games, skating around the frozen Allegheny River on the slick soles of their best shoes. During summer they used the river as their swimming pool. The boys would climb the steel girders of the bridge that separated East Brady from the next town. Walking out to a safe distance from the rugged shoreline, they dropped seventy-five feet into the water, hoping that no jagged rocks lurked just beneath the surface.

But football was always foremost in Jim Kelly's mind. Whenever he grew tired of the drills or wanted to quit, his father knew how to get him back on track again. "Dad looked at the game as my ticket to the future," he said. "And hard work was the only way to get where you wanted to go."

Finally it came time for him to enter East Brady High School. He was following Pat, Ed, and Ray—who already had made a name for themselves on the Bulldogs' football team. No one worried that Jim wouldn't be able to keep up the family gridiron tradition. He was too good *not* to be a star.

Due to low enrollment the team only had twenty-three members. This meant that everybody needed to play more than one position. Besides being a quarterback, Kelly filled in defensively at linebacker, end, and safety. He also did the punting and placekicking. In all of his duties he found the contact part of the game appealed to him most. "Back then, I liked defense the best," he said. "I preferred it to offense because I got the chance to hit people. To me, that was the real purpose of the game."

15

With the start of his sophomore season Jim became the first-string quarterback. He completed 50 percent of his passes for 1,108 yards and 14 touchdowns. The Bulldogs' record was 7–2 for the year. The next year East Brady continued to dominate the Little-12 Conference, a group of small high schools located in central and western Pennsylvania. As a junior, Jim improved his completion percentage to 58 percent while throwing for 1,474 yards and 15 TDs. The team finished with a 9–0–1 record and a share of the league championship.

"We played Clarion-Limestone High School for the title," Jim recalled, "and a victory would have put us alone at the top of the standings. I had a chance to win the game with an extra point, but the kick went wide. So we tied, 13–13, and shared the conference crown. That was the only blemish on an otherwise great season."

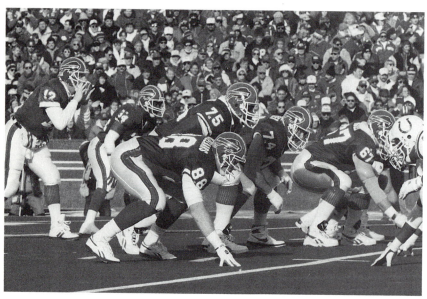

Because Kelly had to play more than one position when he was in high school, he can really understand both the offense and defense. This allows him to be the great quarterback that he is.

As a senior, Jim Kelly threw for 1,333 yards and 15 scores while completing 63 percent of his attempts. He did this even while limited to little more than thirty minutes of playing time each game. "We were usually pretty far ahead of everybody at halftime," Jim explained, "so most of the starters sat out the last two quarters."

The Bulldogs went undefeated, boasting a 10–0 record and becoming the undisputed champions of the Little-12 Conference. Jim's performance for the year also rated special recognition. He was an All-State pick and he received All-America honorable mention. He also became the first player from his league to earn an invitation to the Big-33 East-West All-Star game. This game would be an opportunity to showcase his talents before a number of college recruiters.

When Jim Kelly reported to the West squad, he learned that some of the boys from larger schools were favored by the coaching staff. He started the game at free safety, playing quarterback only a short time. Despite this disappointment, he felt confident that his passing ability was equal to any other quarterback there.

Before he graduated, East Brady High School retired his No. 11 football jersey. It's an honor he cherishes even to this day. Back then, though, his thoughts were taken up with the many college scholarship offers he was receiving. Offers came from such prestigious gridiron powers as Penn State, Pittsburgh, Notre Dame, Tennessee, Kentucky, Georgia, North Carolina State, Maryland, Arizona State, and the University of Miami.

From his earliest days as a football player, Jim had his heart set on playing for Penn State. He religiously followed the Nittany Lions and the team's famous coach Joe Paterno. So when a recruiter from the school said, "We want you," he pictured himself throwing touchdown passes in Beaver Stadium. But this was not what Paterno had in mind.

During a visit to the Penn State campus, Kelly was told that the coaches were interested in him only as a linebacker. He stood 6 feet 3 inches tall and weighed 195 pounds. But Paterno felt that he could bulk up to 235 pounds with the proper training program. Jim Kelly liked the hitting part of the game. He also understood that the Nittany Lions were known for the great linebackers who had played for the team. Still his ambition was to be a quarterback. Not willing to give up his dream, he decided to see what the other colleges thought about him.

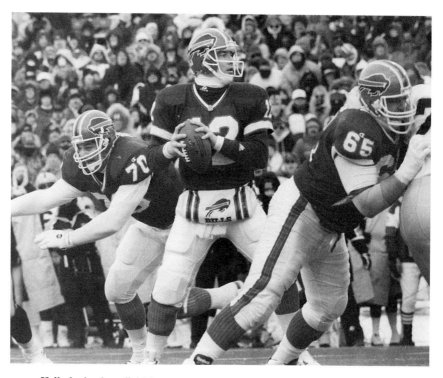

Kelly looks downfield for an open receiver. Becoming a quarterback is what he had always wanted to do.

After listening to promise after promise, he narrowed his choices to Miami and Tennessee. He was quite surprised one snowy day in East Brady when Miami head coach Lou Saban showed up at his front door. They talked long into the night. Jim was filled with visions of sunny Florida beaches, clear blue waters, and a pro-style offense that would make best use of his strong throwing arm. But this beautifully painted picture had a serious flaw. The Hurricanes football fortunes were down—both on the field and at the gate. If the situation didn't get better, the school might drop the sport. Despite this problem, Saban left convinced that he had a new quarterback in the fold.

The following week Kelly traveled to the University of Tennessee for an interview. He was immediately impressed with the size of the school, its modern stadium, and the support the Volunteers football team received from the students. In addition to that, he would be competing for the starting quarterback job as a freshman. All he had to do was sign on the dotted line.

He told the coaches of his promise to Saban. They acted as though he were making a terrible mistake. "Lou Saban's going to leave you stranded there," they said. "Don't you know about him? He doesn't stay in one place very long. Why, he'll probably leave Miami before your sophomore year."

But Kelly had given his word to Saban. He also thought that the Tennessee coaches were just talking in the hope of changing his mind. Nevertheless, he didn't depart from Knoxville without a few regrets. The university had a big-time college football program in which he would have liked to have a part. As for Miami, he really couldn't be sure what to expect.

Chapter 3

Kelly arrived at the University of Miami in August of 1978 for preseason training. His first reaction to the football program was disappointment. Instead of a pro-style passing attack, the Hurricanes used a run-oriented offense. This was not what Coach Saban had promised him.

Jim Kelly learned that he had been "red-shirted" as a freshman. This meant that he would not be allowed to play in regular season games. Instead, he could only practice with the team during the week and watch from the bench on Saturdays. This arrangement *did* give him an extra year to play if he stayed in school, but it wasn't what he'd expected.

To make matters worse, Kelly couldn't even get his old high school number, 11. When he asked for 12—the number worn by his hero Terry Bradshaw—he was told that the number had also been given to someone else. Kelly finally settled for 7, because it was the only quarterback jersey left! Going from the pride of East Brady to just another player at Miami was a huge letdown. He felt like quitting and going home. But his older brother Ray talked him into staying. The advice would turn out to be very good.

Week after week in practice, Kelly handed off to one running back after another. He seldom got a chance to throw the ball and this bothered him. More than once his thoughts turned to Tennessee and how much better it would be playing for the Volunteers. Each time he called his brother Ray to suggest a change, the answer was the same. Ray advised him to be patient and not to jump from the frying pan into the fire.

Kelly quickly learned the difference between high school and college football. At Miami, the players were bigger and faster, and they hit harder. What's more, the time spent studying football was a whole new experience. For hours he watched films of opposing teams, learning to read defenses. Unlike high school, he couldn't just drop back and throw to the open man. Now there were primary receivers and

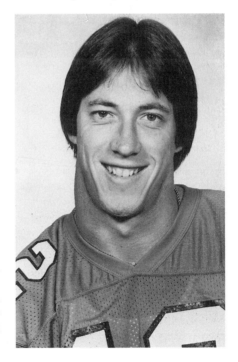

Kelly was in for a few surprises when he first arrived in Miami. Not only was he red-shirted, he couldn't even wear the number that he wanted. But this would soon change.

secondary receivers, depending upon the other team's defensive setup. There was much more strategy involved.

Finally, with the close of the 1978–1979 season, the seemingly endless days of attending "skull sessions" and watching another quarterback get the glory ended. Less than a week later Kelly received a phone call from the athletic department telling him that Saban had left Miami for the U.S. Military Academy at West Point, New York. He was going to coach the Army team.

Could anything else go wrong? Or was it really wrong? Coach Saban hadn't been truthful. The Hurricanes were a running team, not a passing team. Then there was the red-shirt business, which meant a year of sitting on the bench. Once more Kelly called his brother Ray. Again he got good advice: "See who the new head coach is and what kind of an offense he uses. Then make up your mind whether to stay or go."

Very shortly Miami announced that Howard Schnellenberger would take over the football program. He had been offensive coordinator for the Miami Dolphins of the NFL. Before that he was an assistant coach with the Baltimore Colts. In these jobs he had tutored quarterbacks such as the Dolphins' Bob Griese and the Colts' Johnny Unitas. He had also coached Joe Namath and Ken Stabler at the University of Alabama. Kelly began to feel as though there was still hope for him.

Under Schnellenberger, the Hurricanes switched to more of a passing game. As a promising sophomore, Jim Kelly also enjoyed some special treatment at the hands of Earl Morrall. Morrall—a former standout quarterback with the Dolphins, Colts, and New York Giants—was a successful businessperson who had agreed to help coach as a favor to Schnellenberger.

"I look upon Morrall's task as similar to that of a golf pro," Schnellenberger said. "He's to give individual instruction. To help the young quarterbacks develop the techniques they need to succeed in a game situation."

At each practice session Morrall stood at Kelly's elbow, watching his every move. Time and time again he would say, "Reach up, reach up. Put some air under the ball."

Kelly admitted that Morrall did much to make him into a better passer. "I learned to hold the ball higher, which gave me a quicker and more consistent release," he said. "And, too, Morrall taught me to get loft on my passes. That way you can drop the ball into the receiver's hands without him breaking stride."

Morrall knew what a strong arm meant to a quarterback. He also knew that strength could just as easily work against the athlete as for him. One afternoon, following a practice, he discussed the finer points of throwing a football.

A lot of young guys like Jim can put the ball on a line, just zip it in there. Only they have to reach higher before releasing the ball if they're to be successful at this level and as a pro. When those big linemen are rushing in with their hands raised you've got to go over them. If not your passes will be knocked down or picked off. You also have to get some air under the ball for the sake of the receivers. Give them a chance to adjust to it, to use their speed to run under it and away from the defensive player.

With the start of the regular season, Kelly had his jersey number changed to No. 12. He was also listed on the depth chart as the second-string quarterback. Kelly's situation had definitely improved. Then, midway into the Hurricanes' schedule, he got to run the offense in a game for the first time. Kelly came on the field early in the third quarter. Miami was playing against Syracuse University, who was leading, 25–7. After overcoming a case of the jitters, Kelly completed 7 of 17 passes for 130 yards and 1 touchdown. Miami lost, 25–15, but it was a beginning for Kelly.

The following week, Kelly became the first-string quarterback on a permanent basis. The occasion was indeed a special one. Miami was scheduled to play Penn State, the team of Kelly's boyhood dreams. But Penn State was also the team that didn't think he was good enough to run its offense. The coaches had thought he would make a better linebacker. Now Kelly wanted to beat the team, showing the coaches how wrong they were about him.

More than eighty thousand spectators filled Beaver Stadium for the game. Among the fans were Kelly's parents. He intended to make them proud. He did this on Miami's first play from scrimmage, when he threw for a touchdown. His parents continued to cheer as he led the Hurricanes to a 13–10 halftime lead.

During the second-half of play Kelly passed for two more TDs. He finished the afternoon with 18 completions out of 30 attempts for 280 yards and 3 TDs. As a result Miami won easily, 26–10. The victory was a major upset. Kelly had left no doubt in anyone's mind about his ability to be a big-time college quarterback. "I've never seen a quarterback play as well and as poised in his debut as Kelly did today," Coach Schnellenberger told the media.

Success was sweet, but it came with a price. Defenses were now focusing on him. First he had his jaw dislocated. He was then hit in the head and forced to sit out a few plays. Several of his ribs were cracked. But each time Kelly came back stronger than ever. Just as he used to do when his three older brothers gave him a licking. "I took it all as just another challenge," he said of his injuries.

For the final game of the season, Kelly wore a flak vest to protect his damaged ribs. Though it pained him even to

Kelly's first game as starting quarterback was against Penn State—the school of his boyhood dreams.

breathe, he wasn't going to watch from the sidelines. The Hurricanes were playing arch rival University of Florida. Kelly didn't throw as much as usual, just enough to keep the ground attack moving. By the game's end, he had hit 10 of 17 passes for 165 yards and 1 touchdown. Miami won, 30–24, and finished 5–6 for the year.

At the onset of the 1980 campaign, everything came together for Kelly and his teammates. They got off to a fast start, which included a 10–9 win over Florida State. Florida State was then ranked No. 3 in the nation. Once again the Hurricanes ended the season with a victory over the University of Florida, 31–7. In between these games, they lost just three times, compiling an 8–3 record. This record was good enough to rate an invitation to the Peach Bowl.

A near capacity crowd was on hand in Atlanta's Fulton County Stadium. Many fans wanted to see the Hurricanes play

Kelly and his teammates earned an invitation to the Peach Bowl in 1980. The University of Miami beat Virginia Tech, 20–10.

Virginia Tech for the Peach Bowl title. Miami went out front early, and stayed there to win, 20–10. Kelly tossed a 15-yard TD pass and connected with 11 of his 22 aerials for 179 yards total. Attending sportswriters voted him the game's most valuable offensive player.

In 1981 the Hurricanes enjoyed the best of years with a 9–2 record. On the other hand, they suffered the worst of years. This was because recruiting violations kept the team from accepting a major bowl bid. So, although ranked eighth (by the Associated Press) in the country, the team couldn't play in postseason competition and be considered for the national championship. Still, Miami got its share of headlines by registering two major upsets.

The first of these came against Penn State, the No. 1 team in college football. Again Kelly made the Nittany Lions and Coach Joe Paterno wish that they had recruited him as a quarterback. This time, with a cheering Orange Bowl crowd and a national television audience watching, Kelly threw an 80-yard touchdown pass, giving the Hurricanes an early edge. He continued to lead the team to an exciting 17–14 victory.

Powerful Notre Dame became the second upset victim. The occasion was Miami's last game of the season. Kelly got his team out front with a trick play. Instead of being under center, he lined up as a flanker. With the defense keying on him, a wide receiver took the snap and simply trotted into the end zone untouched. The play completely fooled the Irish, who ended up losing, 37–15.

The Hurricanes' offense meshed like a well-oiled machine that day. It rolled for an average 6.3 yards per down and 516 yards overall. Kelly connected with 17 of 25 aerial attempts for 264 yards and 2 TDs. These figures raised his career passing stats to 4,643 yards gained and 29 TDs. Both totals were new Miami records. He still had a season of eligibility left!

By any measure 1982 was supposed to be a big year for Jim Kelly. As a senior and a top quarterback, he became a strong candidate for the coveted Heisman Trophy. This award is given each year to the best college player in the country.

Coach Schnellenberger made no secret about who he thought should win in the voting. "Jim Kelly is the most productive quarterback I've been around," he said. "Our kids have a great deal of confidence in him. Every time he handles the ball, they know they have a chance to score."

Miami opened the season by traveling to Florida State. It was a tough afternoon for the Hurricanes. The Gators regularly used five defenders in the team's secondary to prevent long passing situations. As a result Kelly could only make short throws to his backs and tight ends. The Hurricanes' offense all but ground to a halt, and the team lost, 17–14.

In the Orange Bowl the following week, Kelly and his teammates got back on track against the University of Houston. He connected with 16 of his 27 passing attempts for 208 yards and 1 touchdown. The Hurricanes gained 351 yards overall and a 31–12 victory. Now 1–1, Miami headed north for another away game, feeling confident. But the players' confidence would be shaken again.

For nearly three quarters, Kelly gave his best performance of the young season. He challenged the Virginia Tech defense, gaining 207 yards and 1 TD with a 17 of 24 passing effort. On the third down, from the Miami fourteen, Kelly sprinted out of the pocket in search of a receiver. He saw no one open and decided to run the ball.

Just as he crossed the thirty-yard line, a defender hit him from the side. The force of the blow knocked him to the ground. He fell heavily on his right shoulder. Pain shot through him like an electric shock. He rolled over and tried to lift his throwing arm. It didn't move.

Within a few moments the team doctor was leaning over him, shaking his head. "A total shoulder separation, Jim," the doctor said. "I'm afraid you're done for the season."

The Hurricanes managed to win, 14–8, and Kelly was glad. But the pain made it hard for him to celebrate. Back in Miami, he went to the hospital for surgery. The torn ligaments had to be reattached. Three metal rods were then put in his shoulder to hold everything in place. When he woke up the doctor gave him the bad news. "You might not be able to throw a football again," the doctor said. "If you can do it, fine. But not many people have."

The more Kelly thought about his injury, the more determined he became to play football again. But until the rods were taken out of his shoulder, he could only sit and watch from the bench. It wasn't a pretty sight. The Hurricanes finished with a disappointing 7–4 record. Still Kelly could look with some satisfaction on his own accomplishments.

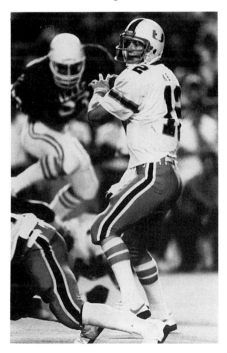

When Kelly was hit by a Virginia Tech defender and separated his shoulder, his doctor said he might never throw again. Kelly was able to prove the doctor wrong.

In little more than two full seasons of play, Kelly had set new school records for the most passing yards (5,228), total offensive yards (5,325), completions (406), and touchdown passes (31).

During this time he started 30 games at quarterback, and Miami won 22 of them. He also earned offensive Most Valuable Player (MVP) honors in each of his nine appearances on national television. While he was calling signals for the team, attendance at the Orange Bowl increased to double what it had been before.

Less than two months after his operation, Kelly began a strenuous rehabilitation program. With the help of the Hurricanes' athletic training staff, he worked long hours every day. He worked at resistance and weight-lifting exercises to strengthen his shoulder. Finally he started throwing again. Only 10 yards at first, then 15, and 20—until he could put the ball downfield with his full strength. This process took about four months.

On April 7, 1983, representatives from all of the NFL clubs were invited to see Jim Kelly go through a series of passing drills. When he walked onto the field several head coaches, twenty pro scouts, and a couple hundred spectators were in the stands. He took his time loosening up in the hot Florida sun. Then, for forty-five minutes, he threw every kind of pass possible: out patterns, square-ins, comebacks, and various short flares and crossing routes. At last he threw four "bombs" of about 70 yards each, completing all of them. There could be no doubt that his arm was as strong as ever.

Dolphins' head coach Don Shula said, "The kid can still throw." A number of scouts agreed that "he had fully recovered from his injury."

Encouraging words, surely; but just words. What the pros really felt about Kelly would be known for certain in a few weeks—when the NFL draft took place.

Chapter 4

The NFL draft was held April 26, 1983. Jim Kelly watched the proceedings on television. He was hoping against hope to be drafted by either the Pittsburgh Steelers or Los Angeles (now Oakland) Raiders. But, to his way of thinking, the worst possibility happened. Buffalo selected him as the 14th pick overall. He definitely did not want to play for the Bills. They had both a losing record and a cold climate.

While his agents negotiated with the United States Football League (USFL) and the Canadian Football League (CFL), Kelly attended Buffalo's minicamp. He was treated well by the coaching staff and the veteran players. The Bills were also willing to give him a four-year contract worth $2.1 million. He began to have better feelings about Buffalo.

But then the USFL came up with a counteroffer. Kelly didn't have to go with the Chicago Blitz, who had taken him in the USFL draft. Instead, he could play with any USFL team of his choice. He would also be paid a lot more money than the Bills had offered. He promptly made a list of three clubs that suited him—the Tampa Bay Bandits, Jacksonville Bulls,

Kelly, in action, against one of the two main teams that he would have liked to have played for when he graduated from Miami—the L. A. (now Oakland) Raiders.

and Houston Gamblers. All of the teams were in warm climates.

In June the Gamblers invited Kelly to Houston. He met with the team owners. When they were satisfied that his shoulder was healed, they offered him a five-year contract for $3.5 million—with a $1 million signing bonus. He didn't hesitate to sign on the dotted line! Suddenly, he was no longer a poor boy trying to make ends meet. The first thing he did was see to the needs of his family.

The Gamblers hired Jack Pardee as head coach. He had been an All-Pro linebacker in the NFL, and later had coached both the Chicago Bears and Washington Redskins. He named Darrel "Mouse" Davis to be the team's offensive coordinator. Davis immediately set about introducing his "run-and-shoot" attack. This meant that Houston was going to throw a lot of short quick passes and put a lot of points on the scoreboard.

At first Kelly didn't like the new plan. He spent hours learning to roll out of the pocket to his right and left. He also had to read defenses and to throw on the run. This was a completely new style of play for Kelly. But he made up his mind to master it. He did all the foot drills to improve his reflexes and whatever else Davis asked.

The first game of the regular season took place in February 1984. Kelly completed 24 of 41 passes for 229 yards and 2 touchdowns. Still, the Gamblers lost to Tampa Bay, 20–17. He had moved the team well, but simply didn't get the ball into the end zone when the opportunities arose.

Against the San Antonio Gunslingers the following week, Kelly put all the offensive pieces together. He threw for 315 yards and 1 TD. He scored twice more while running the ball. This time Houston was the winner, 37–7. Now Kelly felt confident about his ability to be a run-and-shoot quarterback.

Easily, the high point of the season came when he led his team onto the field of Three Rivers Stadium to meet the Pittsburgh Maulers. A dozen buses were needed for fans and friends traveling to the game from East Brady. The game was a homecoming of sorts, and Kelly wanted to do his best. Only the Maulers had other ideas. They sacked him on the first two plays from scrimmage. But Kelly bounced right back to give his best performance of the year. He threw 29 passes, completing 15 of them for 367 yards and 5 touchdowns. The Gamblers won easily, 47–26.

Week after week, the wide-open Houston attack lit up scoreboards around the USFL early and often. Kelly was the man who made plays happen. Sprinting out to one side and the other had become almost second nature to him. He could pass accurately on the move and off either foot. Opposition defenses simply weren't able to adjust fast enough.

At the end of the regular schedule, the Gamblers boasted a 13–5 record and were Western Conference champions. Kelly was named the USFL's Most Valuable Player, and with good reason. He passed for 5,219 yards and 44 touchdowns, averaging at least 1 TD toss every weekend. No less than 9 times he threw for more than 300 yards in a game. It was a super season in any regard.

The run-and-shoot had proved itself to be an awesome offensive weapon. It had a major weakness, though. Because it called for so many receivers to be downfield, there was a lack of blockers to protect the passer. As a result, Kelly took 76 sacks during the 1984 campaign. He also got hit after throwing the ball on practically every down. Many observers wondered how long he would last taking such a pounding. "I don't remember a day during the season that I didn't feel sore," he said.

During his first season in the USFL, Kelly was voted Most Valuable Player. His strong performance in the USFL is what kept Buffalo interested in signing him.

When the playoffs began, Houston lost in the first round to the Arizona Wranglers, 17–16. Kelly played well enough, but he couldn't capitalize on a number of scoring chances. He passed for 301 yards, but failed to throw for any touchdowns. After so much success this was especially disappointing.

Before the start of the 1985 season, the Gamblers challenged the Houston Oilers—the team's NFL neighbor—to play a game. The money from ticket sales would have gone to charity, but the invitation fell on deaf ears. Kelly wasn't surprised. "I had no doubt that we could compete with any NFL club," he said.

In fact the Gamblers drew larger crowds to the Astrodome than did the Oilers. The Gamblers also worked harder at public relations and promotion. Plus the team's black and silver uniforms and an explosive offense that averaged 24 points a game caught the public's fancy. "The fans loved our fighting spirit," Kelly said. "They loved our let's-go-for-it attitude. They loved everything about us."

Mouse Davis left the club early in the year to become head coach of the Denver Gold. But the Houston attack didn't so much as sputter. A lot of the credit for that goes to Kelly. In the opening game of the 1985 season, he took charge. The Los Angeles Express were leading, 33–13, in the fourth quarter. Against the opposition's man-to-man coverage, Kelly suddenly started throwing long instead of staying with the usual quick out and crossing patterns. "It didn't make sense not to use the speed and skills of our receivers," he said. "We just burned them deep."

Only 12 plays and less than 3 minutes were needed to light up the scoreboard and swing the tide of battle. With fleet-footed wideouts Ricky Sanders, Richard Johnson, Gerald McNeil, and Clarence Verdin to do the catching, Kelly hit on touchdown passes of 52, 40, and 39 yards. Overall he had 35 completions out of 54 attempts for 574 yards and 5 TDs. The Gamblers edged out the Express, 34–33.

Houston jumped out to a 5–0 record, with Kelly throwing for an average of 418 yards and 4 touchdowns per game. Then came three losses. One of them was a 31–25 upset at the hands of the New Jersey Generals. The Generals had two Heisman Trophy winners in its lineup—quarterback Doug Flutie and running back Herschel Walker. To make matters worse, the Gamblers nearly lost its star player to an injury.

In the third quarter, Kelly rolled out to his right and got a good rush. Under pressure, he dumped the ball over the middle, just as two defenders collided in front of him. Their helmets banged against his throwing hand, dislocating the ring finger. It was pointing sideways when Kelly was brought into the locker room. After the joint had been straightened, Kelly returned to the game and passed for a touchdown. But the score came too late to prevent defeat.

In every game Kelly took a beating. Finally, in week fourteen, he went down with stretched ligaments in his right knee. He was wheeled from the field, and his leg was placed in a cast. Doctors said that he would miss the rest of the regular season. Without him directing the offense, Houston lost twice more and finished with a 10–8 record.

Kelly made it back for the playoffs. Again, the Gamblers failed to get past the first round. The team dropped a 22–20 decision to the Birmingham Stallions. As before Kelly could only take comfort in his own performance for the year. He was the top-rated quarterback in the USFL, completing 360 of 567 passes for 4,623 yards and 39 TDs. During his first two seasons, he threw for more yards (9,842) and touchdowns (83) than had any quarterback in the history of pro football.

In August officials announced that the USFL was switching from a spring and summer season to a fall schedule.

The change would take place in 1986. Kelly knew some of the teams were having financial problems. So it didn't surprise him too much when the Gamblers merged with the Generals, and he was transferred to New Jersey. There he joined Flutie and Walker on what some sportswriters referred to as a "dream team."

During the spring of 1986 the Generals conducted a week-long minicamp at Giants Stadium in New Jersey. Kelly and his new teammates were upbeat, looking forward to playing in the fall. But that July the USFL came away unsatisfied with the results of its antitrust suit against the NFL. The following month the USFL suspended operations and released all players from their contracts. A quick and exciting ride had come to a sudden end. "I'll always cherish the memories," Kelly said of his USFL experience. "They were two very enjoyable years."

Now the Buffalo Bills team renewed its efforts to sign Kelly. The team still held his rights from the 1983 NFL draft. But Kelly wasn't any more anxious to play for the club than he was years before. He didn't like the climate that far north. And he wasn't happy about going with a team that had been losing steadily for so long. When Kelly heard that the Los Angeles (now Oakland) Raiders were trying to trade for him, he felt his hopes soar. However, the Bills weren't about to lose the chance to get a star quarterback.

Kelly's agents began talking contract with the club representatives. These meetings went on for hours and tempers sometimes wore thin. Often the men got into shouting matches. But at last an agreement was reached. The terms were $8 million to be spread over a period of five years.

When Kelly signed the contract, it made him the highest-paid player in the NFL. He flew to Buffalo for a press conference, and the highway from the airport to downtown

Kelly signed a contract with the Buffalo Bills in 1986 that made him the highest-paid player of the time in the NFL.

was lined with fans. At the hotel where the media had gathered, more people jammed the lobby and loudly cheered him. In the main ballroom the mayor and other dignitaries were on hand to hear his words. He was absolutely amazed at all the attention.

At his first practice session with the team, spectators crowded the area. Reporters and photographers from all over the country were also on hand. His first pass was a 60-yard spiral that hit the receiver right in the hands. The onlookers went wild. Even the coaching staff got excited. Chants of "Kel-lee! Kel-lee!" could be heard. There were signs all over that read "We love you, Jim" and "Welcome Back."

During training camp Kelly studied the Bills' playbook day and night. He talked for hours with offensive coordinator Jim Leahy and head coach Hank Bullough. He watched films both by himself and with the team. He appeared briefly in a couple of exhibition games. Finally, it was time for the regular season to start.

Chapter 5

On Sunday, September 7, 1986, the official head count in Rich Stadium was 79,951. Excitement rippled through the stands like a wave of electricity. Just about everyone there had come to see the Bills' $8-million quarterback make his NFL debut. The occasion marked the beginning of a new era.

The Bills were facing the New York Jets. On Buffalo's first possession, Kelly completed three straight passes. The last one travelled 2 yards to running back Greg Bell for a touchdown and a 7–0 lead. The Jets came back with a pair of TDs, forging ahead, 14–7. A Bills' field goal made the score 14–10. Late in the second period Kelly took an elbow to the head. The hit left him groggy. So, though he managed to finish the half, he didn't remember playing it.

New York's defensive line was in his face all day. But he stayed in the pocket and kept throwing. Just before the third quarter ended, Kelly pitched a 55-yard scoring strike to wideout Andre Reed. Buffalo went ahead, 17–14. Once more New York rallied to get back in front, 28–17.

Never one to quit, Kelly drove the Bills to the Jets' four-yard line. There he started to pass, tripped, then scrambled to his feet. He managed to get the ball to tight end Pete Metzelaars for the TD. The final score was 28–24, Jets. Not a victory for Buffalo, but not a bad first performance by Kelly either.

Buffalo won only 2 out of its first 9 games. As a result Coach Bullough lost his job. Replacing him was Marv Levy, former head coach of the Kansas City Chiefs. He emphasized achieving precision and cutting mistakes to a minimum.

In the first game with Levy on the sidelines, the Bills edged past the Pittsburgh Steelers, 16–12. But Buffalo could do no better than 4–12 for the year. Still, there was a bright spot in this bleak picture. Kelly proved he had the ability to play in the NFL, throwing for a total of 3,593 yards and 22 touchdowns.

The 1987 season rated an asterisk in the record books. After two games, a players' strike was called. Replacement recruits were used by the teams to keep the schedule going.

Buffalo had a losing record his first season there, but Kelly proved that he was a worthy NFL quarterback. He threw for a total of 3,593 yards and 22 touchdowns.

During this temporary arrangement all wins and losses counted in the standings. The walkout lasted five weeks before a settlement was reached. Once back in uniform, the Bills never quite hit their stride, settling for a 7–8 record. But improvement was just around the corner.

Before the 1988 season got underway, Buffalo drafted a young running back named Thurman Thomas. He was just what Kelly needed to take some of the pass-rush pressure off him. Right from the start of the season, the combination worked well together.

Rich Stadium was packed for the opening game against the Minnesota Vikings. The Bills jumped out to a 10–3 lead with a field goal and Thomas's 5-yard scoring run. After another Buffalo field goal, the Vikes closed the gap to 13–10. Late in the final period, Thomas sprinted 28 yards for a critical first down, and the Bills hung on to win.

Kelly dented the Minnesota secondary for 204 yards, but failed to throw a TD pass. The following week Miami also shut him down. He completed 15 of 24 passes for 231 yards, but no touchdowns. Buffalo still managed to eke out a 9–6 victory with three field goals.

Kelly finally broke the end zone ice with a scoring toss at the expense of the New England Patriots. The TD helped the Bills win, 16–14. Against the Pittsburgh Steelers, Kelly completed 20 of 32 throws for 288 yards and a lone TD. So again Buffalo put up just enough points, 36–28, to remain unbeaten.

The Chicago Bears brought the Bills back to earth with a thump, 24–3. The Bears' defense kept Kelly on the move all afternoon, sacking him 6 times. Once more Kelly failed to pass for a touchdown. The Indianapolis Colts also gave him problems and led, 17–7, at the half. But this time Kelly turned the game around in the last two quarters. At the final gun he was 21 of 39 for 315 yards and 3 touchdowns. Buffalo won, 34–23, and improved its record to 5–1.

Everything went right for the Bills and wrong for the Jets. Kelly had a hot hand from the start, throwing two quick scoring strikes of 65 and 66 yards. He hit on 16 of 27 attempts for 302 yards and 3 TDs. Buffalo romped to a 37–14 win. Victories over the New England Patriots, Green Bay Packers, Seattle Seahawks, and Miami Dolphins followed.

When the Jets visited Rich Stadium for a rematch, it was with revenge in mind. The game took place in bitter cold, which made passing difficult. Kelly only connected on 8 of 18 passes, none of which went for a touchdown. At the end of regulation play, the score was 6–6. In overtime the Bills got a field goal that clinched the game, 9–6. The win gave Buffalo the division title.

Immediately afterward, the team dropped 3 of its remaining 4 games. This caused Buffalo to lose its home-field advantage in the playoffs. Still a 12–4 record was quite an accomplishment. The team had done it by running the ball for the most part. How did Kelly feel about throwing only 15 touchdown passes on the season? "I'm a team player," he said. "I just want to win. I don't care how we do it." Coach Levy added, "Jim is a very unselfish football player."

After a week off, Buffalo hosted the Houston Oilers in the divisional round of the playoffs. The game quickly developed into a defensive struggle. A blocked punt provided the Bills with a 7–0 edge. Late in the second half, Buffalo went up, 17–3, on a 10-yard TD run by Thomas and a field goal. From there, the Bills played the Oilers tough to earn a 17–10 victory. This win earned them the chance to play for the American Football Conference (AFC) championship.

Buffalo traveled to Cincinnati, Ohio, for the AFC matchup with the Bengals. In the first quarter Kelly threw two

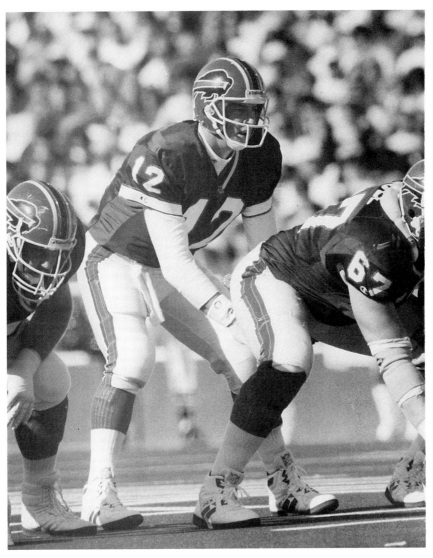

Kelly gets prepared to take the snap. Although known for his passing skills, he is always willing to call running plays to get the ball downfield.

interceptions, the second resulting in a Bengal touchdown. At the top of the second period he completed four successive passes. The last of these was a 9-yard TD strike to Reed, who was running a flare route. This tied the score at 7–7.

The Bills only trailed, 14–10, at the half. But the last thirty minutes of play belonged to the Bengals. Cincinnati won, 21–10, and earned the right to represent the AFC in Super Bowl XXIII.

Jim Kelly had been picked off 3 times. Just 14 of his 30 attempts hit the mark. "I forced a couple of passes I shouldn't have," he told reporters. "We had people open, but I simply didn't make the throws."

Before the 1989 season began, Marchibroda took over as offensive coordinator. The change resulted in the opening up of the Buffalo passing game.

The Bills got the season underway with a road trip to Miami. Less than five minutes remained in the fourth quarter, and the Dolphins led, 24–13. Kelly quickly moved his team downfield to the opposition's twenty-six-yard line. On the next play he hit wide receiver Flip Johnson for a touchdown. The 11-point gap closed to just 4.

An interception gave the Bills the ball at their own twenty-six. The clock showed only 1:44 left to play. With no time-outs, Kelly used a mix of sideline patterns to get the most yardage out of every precious second. Now it was goal-to-go at the Miami two-yard line. Kelly had just one more chance to score a touchdown for the Bills.

In the huddle he called for a flat pass to his right. But when looking at the defense from the shotgun set, he noticed a large hole over the middle. Even as the ball was snapped he said to himself, "I'm going for it." From seven yards deep he sprinted to the open area. A pair of tacklers met him at the goal line. But he lowered his head and burst into the end zone. He had done it again. Final score, 27–24, Buffalo.

Against Denver the following week, the Bills were never in the game, losing 28–14. Kelly completed 26 of 44 passes for 298 yards and 1 touchdown. Houston was the next opponent, and the game proved to be a battle. The lead switched back and forth until an Oilers' field goal made the score 41–41 at the end of regulation play.

In overtime Kelly threw a 28-yard strike for the deciding touchdown. He was at his best that day. His passes hit the mark 17 of 29 times for 363 yards and 5 scores. Next Buffalo manhandled the Patriots, 31–10, to post a 3–1 record. From there it was on the road to Indianapolis.

From the opening kickoff the Colts took charge. The team raced to a 20–0 halftime advantage. Early in the third period Kelly tossed a 16-yard touchdown pass to get the Bills on the

In a game against Miami, with just seconds to go, Kelly noticed a hole and ran with the ball to score the winning touchdown.

47

scoreboard. As he released the ball, a big defensive lineman slammed him to the ground. The result was another separated shoulder—the left one this time. To make matters worse, Buffalo lost, 37–14.

Kelly sat out three weeks. His first game back was a 30–28 loss to the Atlanta Falcons. A 30–7 victory over the Colts followed. But injuries and team morale became a problem in the last part of the schedule. During this time, Buffalo dropped decisions to New England, Seattle, New Orleans, and San Francisco. The Bills won only twice, against Cincinnati and New York, for a 9–7 record. But it was good enough for the AFC Eastern Division title.

The Bills traveled to Cleveland for the second round of the playoffs. In the first thirty minutes Kelly threw touchdown passes of 72 and 52 yards. But the Browns still led, 17–14, at the half. Early in the third quarter Kelly answered an opposition score with one of his own, making the score 24–21, in Cleveland's favor.

After the Browns went up 31–21, Kelly drove his team downfield to score a field goal. Moments later Cleveland also got three points. Kelly countered with a 3-yard touchdown strike. The extra point attempt went wide though, and Buffalo trailed, 34–30.

Late in the fourth period Kelly was knocking at the touchdown door again. As the seconds ticked away, a pass just missed connecting in the end zone. The next pass was intercepted. Once more the Bills were so near, yet so far from the Super Bowl.

Chapter 6

Before the 1990 season began Kelly signed a new contract with the Bills. It was for $20 million, covering a period of six years. The contract was a real vote of confidence from the club. The Bills kept Kelly among the highest-paid quarterbacks in the NFL.

With the start of the new schedule the Buffalo players and coaches felt that this would be a special year. The Colts were the first victim, 26–10. During the Bills' opening series of plays, Kelly completed 9 straight passes using the no-huddle offense. He was 28 of 37 that day throwing for 283 yards and 1 touchdown.

In the next game the Dolphins had a hot hand, winning 30–7. The K-Gun attack produced Buffalo's only score. But the following week the Bills hammered the Jets, 30–7. All of the team's weapons were working to perfection.

The Denver Broncos and the Los Angeles (now Oakland) Raiders visited Rich Stadium for back-to-back contests. With the Broncos leading, 21–9, in the fourth quarter, the Buffalo defense rose to the occasion. A blocked kick, an interception, and a fumble recovery made the final score 29–28, Bills. Los Angeles was up, 24–14, in the final period when Kelly threw a 42-yard TD pass. The defensive unit came to the rescue once again. A blocked punt, a forced fumble, and an interception helped Buffalo to another win, 38–24.

More of the same was in store against the Jets. With the Bills trailing, 27–24, and time running out, Kelly moved the ball 57 yards to the New York fourteen-yard line. The clock showed only 48 seconds left to play. It ticked down to 19 seconds before Kelly found a receiver in the end zone. Buffalo won, 30–27. After throwing for 4 touchdowns that day, he wondered aloud, "Wow! Maybe this is it."

The Bills went on to win four straight, while losing just once. Now the team record was 9–2, with the Philadelphia Eagles coming to Rich Stadium. For this all-important contest the coaching staff decided to use the no-huddle offense the entire game. With Kelly at the K-Gun controls, Buffalo edged Philadelphia, 30–23.

Indianapolis fell, 31–7, and the New York Giants were next in line. The Giants scored first, but Kelly brought the Bills right back with completions of 48 and 6 yards to tie the score at 7–7. Minutes later he drove his team to another touchdown. Just before the half, though, he injured his left knee and had to leave the game. An examination in the locker room determined that he would be out three to six weeks. Buffalo hung on for the victory, 17–13.

Kelly could only walk the sidelines and watch his backup, Frank Reich, direct the Bills to a 24–14 win over Miami and the AFC Eastern Division title. Buffalo closed the season with a 29–14 loss to the Washington Redskins, finishing at 13–3 for the year.

All this time Kelly was strengthening his knee in hope of playing again. He was ready when the Dolphins came to town for the divisional round. On the Bills' first possession of the game, Kelly drove the team to a score in just four plays. The payoff was a 30-yard pitch to Reed. Buffalo led, 7–0.

In the second period Kelly connected with a 17-yard touchdown toss. The Bills led, 27–17, at the half. A Miami touchdown made the score 27–24 at the top of the third quarter. Kelly went back to work, guiding his team to a pair of scores. The last one was the result of a 26-yard pass. Kelly was 19 of 29 for 339 yards and 3 touchdowns. Buffalo won the game, 44–34.

Cold and snow greeted the Raiders' arrival at Rich Stadium for the AFC Championship game. Again the Bills used the no-huddle offense. This time Kelly had it running in high gear. Early in the first period he dropped a snap,

The Colts were the first of the many Bills' victims during the 1990 season.

recovered the fumble, and threw 13 yards for a touchdown. Buffalo led, 7–0.

The Raiders came back with a field goal, then watched the Bills run up 44 points. Kelly was never sacked while hitting on 17 of 23 passes for 300 yards and 2 touchdowns. His completion percentage of 73.9 set a new AFC Championship game record. But most importantly, Buffalo won, 51–3. Super Bowl XXV was next.

Tampa Stadium in Florida hosted the big game. The Giants, looking to square accounts, were the National Football Conference (NFC) representatives. After a first-quarter New York field goal, Kelly put the Bills in scoring position with a 61-yard strike to wide receiver James Lofton. Buffalo also had to settle for a field goal, though. The score was tied, 3–3.

In the second period Kelly kept the Giants guessing while driving his team 80 yards for a touchdown. A few minutes later Buffalo defensive end Bruce Smith caught New York quarterback Jeff Hostetler in his own end zone for a safety. The Bills went ahead, 12–3. Just before the half ended a Giant's touchdown narrowed the count to 12–10, Buffalo.

In the third quarter another score put the Giants ahead, 17–12. But Kelly brought the Bills back with a second touchdown drive. Buffalo went ahead, 19–17, when Thomas broke loose on a 31-yard run to the New York goal line. In the fourth period the Giants kicked a field goal to regain the lead, 20–19.

With just two minutes and sixteen seconds left in the game, Kelly tried to rally his team once more. He started at the Buffalo ten-yard line and worked the ball to the New York twenty-nine, using a mix of runs and short passes. Only seconds remained. Bills' kicker Scott Norwood came out to attempt a 47-yard field goal. The ball sailed wide, and the Giants were Super Bowl champions.

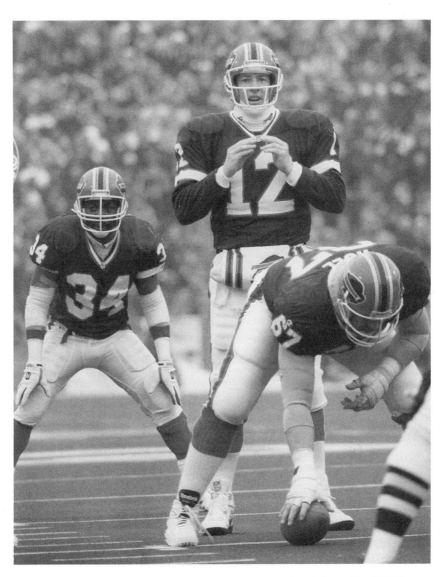

Kelly and the Bills crushed the Raiders 51–3, earning a place in Super Bowl XXV.

No one talked in the Buffalo locker room until Coach Levy said quietly, "There's not one loser here. So, guys . . . just hang in there."

The Bills did hang in there. They put together another 13–3 record during the 1991 season. Buffalo also claimed its fourth AFC Eastern Division title in a row. Without any serious injuries, Kelly was at his best.

Buffalo hosted Miami in the opening game for both teams. The Dolphins jumped to a 14–0 lead before Kelly got the Bills going with a 54-yard touchdown strike. He left in the third period with a slightly sprained ankle. He returned shortly, throwing a 50-yard touchdown pass. He was 29 of 39 for 381 yards and 2 scores. Buffalo won, 35–31.

The Steelers visited Rich Stadium next. Kelly greeted them with 6 touchdown tosses. He completed touchdown passes of 53, 34, 14, 14, 11, and 4 yards, as the Bills routed Pittsburgh, 53–34. The K-Gun had never worked better.

A pair of road games followed. The Jets led, 20–16, late in the fourth period. But Kelly drove his team for the needed score. His 15-yard TD pass gave Buffalo a 23–20 win. He also saved the day again against the Tampa Bay Buccaneers. With the score 10–10 in the last quarter, Kelly connected on a 29-yard pay dirt pitch. The touchdown was the margin of victory for the Bills, 17–10.

Back at Rich Stadium the Bears came calling. Kelly got Buffalo out front, 7–6, with a 33-yard completion just before the first half ended. He also added scoring throws of 2 and 77 yards. The day's win, 35–20, helped the Bills to stay unbeaten. Kelly's play earned him his third 300-yard performance in 5 games.

Defense and a strong running attack sparked the Kansas City Chiefs to a 33–6 upset of Buffalo on *ABC's Monday Night Football*. Kelly was sacked 6 times, which resulted in 3 costly turnovers. Afterward he said, "It was just one of those games where they did everything right, and everything we did seemed to backfire."

Next the Colts invaded Rich Stadium. Early in the first quarter the defense sent Kelly to the sidelines with a mild concussion. Still, the Bills won easily, 42–6. The following weekend Kelly returned to the lineup and threw 5 touchdown passes. Buffalo crushed the Bengals, 35–16.

Buffalo finished the 1991 season with wins over New England, Green Bay, Miami, New York, Los Angeles, and Indianapolis. The team suffered only 2 losses, to New England and Detroit.

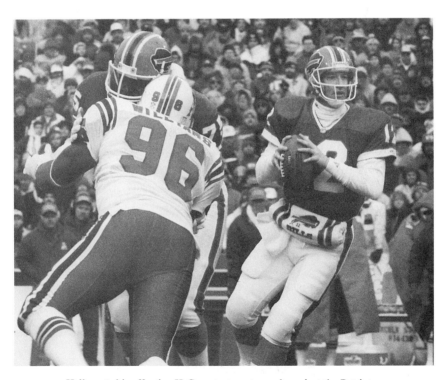

Kelly puts his effective K-Gun strategy to work against the Patriots.

In the divisional round of the playoffs Jim Kelly got even with the Chiefs. Before a capacity crowd at Rich Stadium he pitched a 25-yard touchdown strike. The score gave Buffalo a 7–0 first-quarter edge. Kelly then added touchdown passes of 53 and 10 yards. The Bills won easily, 37–14.

A week later Denver came to Rich Stadium for the AFC Championship game. The matchup was a defensive struggle all the way. Buffalo's only touchdown resulted from a pass interception. That runback, plus a field goal, enabled the Bills to eke out a 10–7 victory.

Super Bowl XXVI took place at the Metrodome in Minneapolis, Minnesota. The NFC Champion Redskins were in Kelly's face all afternoon. He was sacked 5 times and threw 4 interceptions. In the last quarter a blow to the head sidelined him for a few plays. Still, he came back for more.

Washington led, 37–10, before Kelly finally connected with touchdown tosses of 2 and 4 yards. But it was too little and way too late. Buffalo came up short again in the big one, losing 37–24.

Kelly had to be helped from the field. When talking to reporters he could only say, "I don't remember much. But the part I can remember I don't like."

Kelly began the 1992 season with a hot hand. He directed the Bills to a 40–7 victory over the Los Angeles (now St. Louis) Rams at Rich Stadium. On that day he completed 13 of 19 passes for 106 yards and a pair of touchdowns.

Next Buffalo was on the road to San Francisco. Kelly shredded the 49ers defense with 22 of 33, passing for 303 yards and 1 touchdown. The Bills won, 34–31. Back home against the Colts, Kelly was 17 of 27 for 211 yards and 2 scores. Buffalo shut out Indianapolis, 38–0.

At New England the following week, Kelly threw for 3 touchdowns, and the Bills battered the Patriots, 41–7. Two games in the loss column followed. Miami won, 37–10, as did the Raiders, 20–3. In both outings Kelly passed for more than 300 yards.

The Bills got back on track with victories over the Jets, Patriots, Steelers, Dolphins, and Falcons. Despite this run of success Kelly was having problems. He had begun throwing more interceptions than touchdowns. Both the Colts and the Jets picked him off twice while winning, 16–13, and 24–17, respectively.

Buffalo edged Denver, 27–17, and New Orleans, 20–16, before losing the season's final game to Houston, 27–3. The Broncos nabbed 2 of Kelly's passes, while the Saints and Oilers stole 1 each. Kelly ended the year with a league-high

Kelly is getting ready to pass during the Bills' third straight Super Bowl.

19 interceptions. To make matters worse, he had badly sprained his right knee.

For the first time in five years the Bills, at 11–5, did not win the AFC Eastern Division crown. The team entered the playoffs as a wild card. Houston was Buffalo's first-round opponent. The Bills fell behind, 35–3, early in the third period. Kelly could only watch from the sidelines, his knee heavily bandaged. But the Bills mounted a miraculous comeback to beat the Oilers in overtime, 41–38.

Kelly also sat out the next week as Buffalo whipped Pittsburgh, 24–3. When it came time to face the Dolphins for the AFC Championship, Kelly was ready to go. In the second quarter he put the Bills ahead, 10–3, with a 17-yard touchdown pass. From there the team went on to an easy 29–10 win. The Bills were going to the Super Bowl for the third straight year. "I think this team has really matured a lot," Kelly said, "and is ready to go out and win a Super Bowl."

Nearly one hundred thousand spectators were on hand when Buffalo and the NFC champion Dallas Cowboys met in Pasadena, California, for Super Bowl XXVII. The score was 7–7 in the first period when Jim Kelly fumbled, and the Cowboys turned it into a touchdown. At the top of the second quarter Kelly drove the Bills to the Dallas one-yard line. On fourth down he threw an interception. Shortly afterward he reinjured his right knee and left the game for good.

From that point Dallas quickly expanded a small 14–10 lead into a lopsided 52–17 victory. But 30 of these points could be traced directly to 9 Buffalo turnovers. The Bills' play was a classic case of a team being its own worst enemy. "You turn the ball over the way we did, there's no way you're going to win the game," Kelly said.

Once again the cry could be heard, "Wait until next year."

The 1993 schedule got underway with Buffalo winning big at home against New England, 38–14. Kelly threw for 4 touchdowns but only 167 yards. At Dallas the next week he was 16 of 27 for 155 yards and 1 touchdown. Without All-Pro running back Emmitt Smith, the Cowboys lost, 13–10.

Despite these successes Kelly was still struggling with interceptions. He had been picked off once in each game. The Dolphins then stole 2 of his passes, beating the Bills, 22–13. A week later the Giants intercepted him but still came up short, 17–14.

Buffalo's record improved to 7–1 with wins over the Oilers, Jets, Redskins, and Patriots. Although the no-huddle offense was sputtering, Kelly was playing better. He passed for 3 touchdowns against Houston and 2 more at the expense of Washington.

At Pittsburgh, the Bills were blanked, 23–0. Kelly only connected with 7 of 19 attempts for 93 yards.

In a 23–9 victory over the Colts, Kelly was 19 of 27 for 224 yards and 2 touchdowns. Losses to Kansas City and the Raiders followed. In these 2 games he threw a total of 4 interceptions. Now Buffalo's record stood at 8–4.

To be sure of a home-field advantage, the Bills needed to win their last four games. They did, beating the Eagles, Dolphins, Jets, and Colts for AFC Eastern Division honors. For the season, Kelly threw just 18 touchdown passes and the same number of interceptions.

Buffalo hosted the Raiders in the divisional round, edging Los Angeles 29–23. Kelly made the difference with a pair of touchdown pitches in the second half. When the Chiefs came to Rich Stadium the next weekend for the AFC Championship game, the Bills were ready. They used a tough defense and a strong running attack to whip the Chiefs, 30–13.

"Every time Jim handed me the ball, he'd yell 'Go!'," said Thomas, who rushed for an impressive 186 yards. "He knew I would do well today."

During the first half of Super Bowl XXVIII at the Georgia Dome in Atlanta, it looked as though an upset was in the making. A pair of field goals and a 4-yard run gave Buffalo a 13–7 halftime lead. But at the top of the third period the Cowboys returned a fumble for a touchdown to tie the score at 13–13.

Early in the fourth period with Dallas ahead, 20–13, Kelly drove his team deep into enemy territory. An interception ruined any comeback hopes though. The Cowboys notched another touchdown and a field goal while holding the Bills scoreless. Dallas won, 30–13. Kelly gave his best effort,

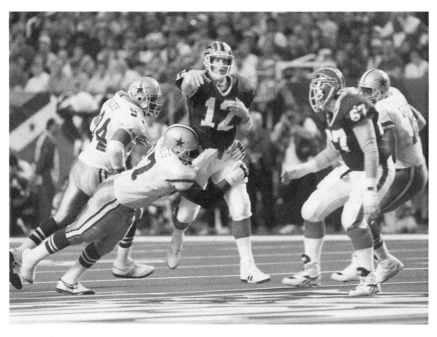

With the Cowboys' defense close at hand, Kelly passes in Super Bowl XXVIII. This would be Buffalo's fourth straight loss in the Super Bowl.

completing 31 of 50 passes for 260 yards. But the Cowboys' defense simply kept him on the run all afternoon. "I feel bad," he said afterward. "I've been here four times. It's frustrating, it really is, but I have a couple of years left yet. So don't count me out."

Going into the 1994 season he had thrown for more than 25,000 yards. Few other quarterbacks in the history of the NFL have done as well. Still his thoughts are fixed on the future and winning a Super Bowl. "We [Bills] will just have to keep trying," he said. "We'll have to figure out a way to get the job done." The future will surely bring new challenges for Kelly.

Jim Kelly is not a man to be counted out.

Career Statistics

YEAR	TEAM	PASSING				RUSHING			
		PASS ATT.	PASS COMP.	PASS YARDS	TDs	ATT	YDS	AVG	TDs
1984	Houston	587	353	5,219	44	85	493	5.8	5
1985	Houston	567	360	4,623	39	28	170	6.1	1
USFL Totals		1,154	713	9,842	83	113	663	5.9	6
1986	Buffalo	480	285	3,593	22	41	199	4.9	0
1987	Buffalo	419	250	2,798	19	29	133	4.6	0
1988	Buffalo	452	269	3,380	15	35	154	4.4	0
1989	Buffalo	391	228	3,130	25	29	137	4.7	2
1990	Buffalo	346	219	2,829	24	13	72	5.5	0
1991	Buffalo	474	304	3,844	33	20	45	2.3	1
1992	Buffalo	462	269	3,457	23	31	53	1.7	1
1993	Buffalo	470	288	3,382	18	36	102	2.8	0
1994	Buffalo	448	285	3,114	22	25	77	3.1	1
NFL Totals		3,942	2,397	29,527	201	259	972	3.8	5

Where to Write Jim Kelly

Mr. Jim Kelly
Jim Kelly Enterprises, Inc.
Main Place Tower/Suite 200
Buffalo, New York 14202

Index

A

ABC's Monday Night Football, 54
American Football Conference
      (AFC), 44, 46, 48, 50, 51,
      52, 54, 56, 58, 59
Arizona Wranglers, 36
Atlanta Falcons, 48, 57

B

Baltimore Colts, 22
Beaver Stadium, 18
Bell, Greg, 41
Birmingham Stallions, 37
Bradshaw, Terry, 14, 20
Brown, Jerome, 7, 10, 12
Bulldogs, 15, 17
Bullough, Hank, 40, 42

C

Canadian Football League, (CFL), 31
Chicago Bears, 33, 43, 54
Chicago Blitz, 31
Cincinnati Bengals, 44, 46, 48, 55
Clarion-Limestone High School, 16
Cleveland Browns, 48

D

Dallas Cowboys, 58, 59, 60, 61
Davis, Darrel "Mouse", 33, 36
Denver Broncos, 47, 49, 56, 57

E

East Brady, Pa., 13, 15, 16, 20, 34
East Brady High School, 14, 15, 17
East-West All-Star Game, 17

F

Florida State, 26, 28
Flutie, Doug, 37, 38

Fulton County Stadium, 26

G

Georgia Dome, 60
Giants Stadium, 38
Green Bay Packers, 44
Griese, Bob, 22

H

Hiesman Trophy, 28, 37
Hostetler, Jeff, 52
Houston Gamblers, 33, 34, 36, 37, 38
Houston Oilers, 36, 44, 47, 57, 58
Hurricanes, 19, 20, 22, 23, 24, 26,
      27, 28, 29, 30

I

Indianapolis Colts, 43, 47, 48, 49,
      50, 55, 57, 59

J

Johnson, Flip, 46
Johnson, Richard, 36
Joyner, Seth, 7, 12

K

K-Gun, 8, 9, 11, 49, 50, 54
Kansas City Chiefs, 42, 54, 56, 59
Kelly, Alice, 13
Kelly, Danny, 13
Kelly, Ed, 13, 15
Kelly, Joe, 13, 14
Kelly, Kevin, 13
Kelly, Pat, 13, 15
Kelly, Ray, 13, 15, 21, 22

L

Leahy, Jim, 40
Levy, Marv, 8, 42, 44, 54
Little-12 Conference, 16, 17
Lofton, James, 8, 10, 11, 52

Los Angeles Express, 36
Los Angeles (Oakland) Raiders, 31, 38, 49, 50, 51, 52, 55, 57, 59
Los Angeles (St. Louis) Rams, 56

M

Marchiboda, Ted, 8, 9, 46
McNeil, Gerald, 36
Metzelaars, Pete, 42
Miami Dolphins, 22, 30, 43, 46, 49, 50, 51, 54, 55, 57, 58
Minnesota Vikings, 43
Morrall, Earl, 22, 23

N

Namath, Joe, 22
National Football Conference, (NFC), 52, 56
National Football League (NFL), 7, 30, 31, 33, 36, 38, 42, 49, 61
New England Patriots, 43, 47, 48, 55, 56, 57, 59
New Jersey Generals, 37, 38
New Orleans Saints, 48, 57
New York Giants, 22, 50, 55, 59
New York Jets, 41, 42, 44, 50, 54, 57, 59
Nittany Lions, 17, 18, 27
no-huddle offense, 8, 51, 59
Norwood, Scott, 9, 11, 52

O

Orange Bowl, 27, 28, 30

P

Pardee Jack, 33
Paterno, Joe, 17, 27
Peach Bowl, 26
Penn State, 17, 18, 24, 27
Philadelphia Eagles, 6, 7, 8, 9, 10, 12, 50, 59
Pittsburgh Maulers, 34

Pittsburgh Steelers, 14, 31, 42, 43, 54, 57, 58, 59

R

red-shirt(ed), 20, 22
Reed, Andre, 9, 11, 41, 46
Reich, Frank, 50
Rich Stadium, 7, 41, 44, 49, 50, 54, 55, 56, 59
run-and-shoot, 33, 34

S

Saban, Lou, 19, 20, 22
Sanders, Ricky, 36
San Francisco 49ers, 48, 56
Schnellenberger, Howard, 22, 24, 28
Seattle Seahawks, 44, 48
Shula, Don, 30
Simmons, Clyde, 7, 12
Smith, Bruce, 52
Smith, Emmitt, 59
Stabler, Ken, 22
Super Bowl, 11, 46, 48, 52, 56, 57, 58, 60, 61
Syracuse University, 23

T

Tampa Bay Bandits, 31, 33
Tampa Bay Bucaneers, 54
Thomas, Thurman, 7–8, 9, 10, 43, 52, 60
Three Rivers Stadium, 14, 34

U

Unitas, Johnny, 22
United States Football League (USFL), 31, 34, 37, 38

V

Verdin, Clarence, 36

W

Walker, Herschel, 37, 38
Washington Redskins, 33, 50, 56, 59
White, Reggie, 7, 12